HAPPY
SCHOOL
YEAR!

HAPPY SCH

by SUSAN MILORD

OOL YEAR!

Illustrations by MARY NEWELL DePALMA

Scholastic Press / New York

All over town,
children are
waking up.

Some open their eyes
with the morning light,
while others turn off
noisy alarms.

Some are woken by parents,
some by brothers and sisters,
grandmothers and uncles.

Some of the children
bound out of bed.
Others yawn and stretch and squint
through half-opened eyes.

One child burrows under
the covers, hiding until
the last possible minute.

Some children
hear water running
and throats gargling
and hair dryers blowing.

Others listen to a distant radio
and the sounds only
a kitchen makes.

All over town, children
are starting their day.

But this is not just any day.

Today is the first day of school.

One by one,
the children get dressed.
Many choose new
jeans or jumpers,
T-shirts or tops.

One child has shoes

put back on

the right feet.

A few of the children
eat breakfast alone,
while others slip into
the last chair at busy tables.
Some talk excitedly
about the day ahead.

One child worries about morning snack.

After breakfast,
the children
brush their teeth
and wash their faces
and comb their hair.

They fill backpacks and pockets
with lunches and pencils
and crayons and notebooks
and special reminders of home.
After many kisses and hugs,
it is time to leave for school.

Some children walk or ride bicycles,
while others roll along on scooters
and skateboards.

Many arrive in shiny cars or tumble from big
yellow buses. A few trail behind brothers
and sisters, moms and dads.

In the school yard,

lots of children rush to join friends.

Others cling to their parents.

Some hold back tears.

One child thinks about running away.

Then a loud bell rings,
and everyone moves through the front doors,
down stairs and along hallways

and around corners,
to an enormous room, where the teachers
and staff are waiting.

The principal raises her hand for quiet and
welcomes everyone to school.

"A new school year is a great adventure," she says,
"and like all great adventures,
it can sometimes be a little scary.

"But we are all here to help one another.
And I think you'll find friends
along the way."

Then she asks everyone to make
a wish for the school year
as she counts to three.

"One,"

the principal says softly.

Each child thinks

of a wish.

"Two,"

the principal says.

There are no more thoughts

about hiding or running away,

no more worries about shoes

or morning snack.

"Three!

"HAPPY SCHOOL YEAR!"

The cheers of two hundred nine

students and their parents,

twenty-six teachers and staff, and

one principal fill the room.

"*Happy school year for us,*" someone sings.

"*Happy school year for us,*"

children and parents and teachers chime in.

"May this be the best ever,
Happy school year for us!"

Go Fish

And by the time
the song is over,
everyone knows
it will be just that.

⫿⫿⫿⫿⫿ A NOTE ON THE CELEBRATION ⫿⫿⫿⫿⫿

First Day of School events like the one shown in this book happen in thousands of communities across the United States. They bring together students, parents, teachers, administrators, and community members to celebrate the joy of learning, the importance of education, and the beginning of another happy school year!

A First Day celebration starts with the school, which organizes activities for families and community members. Parents make a commitment to attend; employers allow working parents time off to participate. And then parents, teachers, and administrators have the chance to build relationships starting from day one. Everyone – especially students – benefits from the improved communication and the demonstrated community support for education resulting from these activities.

The First Day campaign began in 1997, when eleven schools in the Southwest Vermont Supervisory Union held a successful First Day celebration and decided to make it an annual tradition. A magazine publisher named Terry Ehrich established the First Day Foundation to spread the word and inspire other schools to join the campaign. Today thousands of schools host First Day celebrations for families and students in grades kindergarten through high school.

For more information or a First Day Activity Guide,
please visit the First Day Foundation Web site at www.firstday.org.

Library of Congress Cataloging-in-Publication Data
Milord, Susan.
Happy school year! / by Susan Milord ; illustrated by Mary Newell DePalma. – 1st ed.   p. cm.
Summary: Children gather for a first day of school celebration that calms their worries about the day.
Includes note about the history of such celebrations, and a related website.
ISBN 978-0-439-88280-4
[1. First day of school–Fiction. 2. Schools–Fiction.] I. DePalma, Mary Newell, ill. II. Title.
PZ7.M6445Hap 2008   [E]–dc22   2007021472
ISBN-13: 978-0-439-88280-4 / ISBN-10: 0-439-88280-X
10 9 8 7 6 5 4 3 2 1   08 09 10 11 12
Printed in Singapore 46 / First edition, July 2008

The display type was set in Eetwell Bold. The text was set in Minya Nouvelle Regular.
The art was created using acrylic paint on watercolor paper. Book design by Elizabeth B. Parisi & Patty Harris